FROM THE DEER FOREST

A Story of Wolves

by G. Lowell Tollefson

FROM THE DEER FOREST

A Story of Wolves

by G. Lowell Tollefson

I

A wolf's life begins in May; and in the Northwest coast country, centuries before America was discovered by Europeans, a litter of six was born in the rain forest that lined the north bank of what is now known as the Hoh river. The den was located under the thrust up roots of a big, old maple that had been toppled by winds. The mewling pups, less than three days old, could not see, and it was enough work to tumble about in the dark, warm tunnel against the bitch wolf's body, grappling in search of a teat.

All the pups were of a tannish hue, but the subject of our story, one of two males, was a little darker, grayer. He was also slightly larger than his brother, gaining thereby an advantage at the dinner board, but was a bit smaller than his four hulking and less energetic sisters.

The bitch had not left them from the moment of their birth, arising only to urinate at various chosen points near the mouth of the den, then returning to them. All her needs were well provided for, her mate returning on an average of once a day in the early morning to regurgitate the night's haul in vermin and an occasional fawn. Theirs was always an affectionate reunion, and there was much whimpering and caressing of muzzles before the male retreated to a knoll overlooking the river through dense forest a few yards from the den.

The forest was everywhere, dense, heavily hung in moss that blanketed the thick branches of the great maples, and dark.

A dense growth of trees and brush crowded up to the very edge of the river and ran alongside it so thickly, the big male could not have seen anything from his knoll, though his sight was keen. But his hearing was even keener, and nothing large enough to be a threat, not even a stealthy bobcat or puma, could move through the underbrush of the river bank without attracting his attention. A keen sense of smell also served him well, and, by means of the acrid, clean odor of the damp rain forest, assaulted him with pleasant dreams as he slept away most of his day.

The bitch, when marking her favorite signposts with urine in front of the den, did not have to descend to the river to slake her thirst. A small, slow moving stream, almost a pool, clear as winter ice, lay in a rivulet along the gently sloping hillside just above the den. This was one of the many trickles that met in the greater flood of the river. The humus and rotting logs that lay about it were rich in salamanders and insects, and the she wolf occasionally caught a small frog in one of its eddies. But there were no fish. The water was not deep enough, the spring too near the mighty river to attract adventurers from its passing flow.

In nine days the pups were able to see. Gray, for so we shall call the darker male, was aware of a waxy display of soft shadows which seemed now never to leave him but in sleep. The great source of warm milk and the gentle tongue that bathed him and took away the soiling he left in the nest, was the largest moving shadow. Other, smaller ones fought him in a topsy-turvy tumble sort of way for his chance at a teat. This was knowledge which he quickly learned to use in getting a meal. Being the smallest and most energetic, since his brother had died and been removed from the nest two days before, he had to rely upon his special gifts of quickness and energy to overcome the blockades and inroads of his burly sisters.

The apperception of sight brings another element into the life of a being. It makes him aware that his other senses, smell and hearing for example, not to mention touch and the opposition of heat and cold, are related to objects having separate, concrete existences.

It would not do to say that Gray was at this point responsive to his sisters as individuals like himself. They were only so many accumulations or stoppages in the artery of life, blocking the flow of his will. Even his mother was simply a focal point of impulse and satisfied need.

But clarity came to the blue eyes of the young pup, as it did to his sisters, and their legs grew stronger until they discovered that there was a kind of sequential rolling of the feet that proved much more effective in getting results than rolling loosely on one's back, like a barrel. Of course, the desired result was still an access to warm milk. But they were also able at three weeks to pad about the den and venture not too near the entrance but close enough to catch a glimpse of blinding light between the tangled roots of the fallen tree. This was a strange thing, this light. For it retreated and came, waxed and waned with the passing hours. A growing curiosity about it seized Gray and his sisters, but they did not get a chance to make the discovery themselves.

It was at about this time that their mother suddenly introduced them to the full light of day. A rude awakening it was, as the forest was dripping with rain, which they had not yet learned was a common event. The den having become too crowded as the pups grew larger, she had chosen to remove them to higher ground above the spring. Here beneath a small opening in the canopy of the forest, near the trunk of another fallen tree blanketed in moss and covered with yellow, orange and cream colored fungi, she hid the pups in dense underbrush that had sprung up in the sudden access to light. They were able to get out of most of the rain by cringing in a close packed ball beneath the curve of the log and shivering together like a ripple of grasses, but this was certainly not like home. Yet it toughened them, for they had soon grown quite accustomed to it—yes, even the rain! They would gambol about, shaking the water, when it came, off their smooth, oily coats and slaking their thirst by licking themselves dry. Mother came and went. Father also came and went. Both parents were now feeding them regurgitated meat, slowly weaning them from milk, so they were often left alone for short stints.

When this happened, they did not venture out to see what was doing while mom and pop were off. They crowded together in a furry ball and awaited the elders' return. But the bitch never went far. Only the male would be gone for the night, sometimes for several days now.

One day Gray lost a sister. They were about seven weeks old and used to gamboling about quite freely in the presence of their parents, even leaving the nest site and venturing into the open in play. The clearing they occupied was not large; certainly it was insufficient in size to serve as a regular hunting ground for a large bird of prey. But a goshawk, that normally worked some small islets in the Hoh river, had come to rest in one of the nearby trees. The pups had gamboled out of the brush in pursuit of their mother as she darted off to greet their approaching father. They could not keep up with her and were also afraid to venture too far from the nest. But they did not all return to cover quickly enough. Several of them, including

Gray, had stood in the open momentarily, tails crooked downward, howling mournfully.

The hawk, with its sharp, roving eye and quick moving head, spotted them. It dropped from the crown of the tree where it was perched, flapped its wings heavily three or four times and descended silently, like an arrow, upon them. Gray felt the shadow, rather than saw it. He turned tail, as did the other two pups who were with him. But the shadow blackened, resolved in a flurry of wings, and a single high pitched cry of triumph announced to the frightened pups, four of them now cowering together against the log, that the thing was done.

When the bitch returned, followed closely by her mate, she seemed a little more anxious than usual as she nuzzled and licked her pups. But soon she settled in to nurse, and the big male, not having brought a meal, retreated off a little distance to take his rest.

There is perhaps nothing more thrilling than the sound of the male wolf's high bugle call in the inky black night of the forest. It drifts in from afar, and the bitch pricks her ears, beginning to whine anxiously and moving about, breaking free of the suckling pups. Then she leaves them, ascends to a slightly higher elevation and returns the call. The single pitch treble, so high, thin and fine sounding, is the call to form up for the hunt. But this is usually only done in winter, when the game becomes scarcer and larger on the average, requiring more than one predator to bring it down. Acting thus in concert, the wolves are able to subsist on larger game, like elk and deer, while the summer fare of small mammals, amphibians and reptiles becomes less active or hibernates underground.

But even when there is no pack to be formed, the male will bugle for his mate, and she will answer, breaking into the sharp yawps that are a sound of recognition and bonding to his ears.

Gray heard these calls often in the night, knew his mother had gone to answer them, and wondered what the meaning was of the excitement that ran thrillingly through his body, sometimes raising the hair about his neck. He had a great yearning to be off somewhere doing something urgent, but had not the least understanding of what it was.

By the time the pups were several months old the mother was often away at night hunting with the father. Larger game was required to feed the growing bodies of the hungry pups, and two hunters now made better provision than one. The summer days were hot; and, though the nights were cooler, the softer weather enhanced the pups' nervous energy. They huddled together near the log and did not dare to go forth in the dark, but they were often awake through the long hours. Both mother and father came at regular intervals in the daytime to regurgitate food. But the mother had weaned them from milk, snapping irritably at them when they still piled pell-mell over one another to get their unpleasantly sharp little teeth on a teat.

Sometimes the father would remain with the pups during the day while the mother went off hunting. Whenever either parent was about in the light of morning and afternoon, the pups were allowed to ramble here and there, foraging for grubs, beetles, frogs or salamanders. These were glorious times, full of wild scents and sweet odors.

II

One day the mother, acting peculiarly anxious, whining and coaxing, led the whole litter down the bank toward the river. Though the spring flood had abated, the river was still strong and deep in August, and the sun sparkled blindingly over these waters which the pups saw for the first time.

There is something of the wild, Northwestern river, with its fresh, white foaming urgency, the clean smell of its spray, the occasional salmon or trout breaking surface, and the gray dipper bird bobbing on a rock and descending into a pool, that sends a quiver through one's veins and makes him young. For such rivers do not glide; they roar and dash over smooth, slate colored rocks, and the pebbly bottom near their edges is clearly visible. Here minnows dart about in pools where the rocks are sufficiently protected from the sun to gather moss and the water calm enough to produce algae with the accompanying small animal life that feeds them. Cedar, hemlock and fir soar lush, rich and dark along the banks. The blue sky is made ever bluer by the intense green of the forest, and there is rarely a cloud in it on warm August days, once the white, morning fog has lifted. It is the loveliest, freest time of year in rain forest country.

The bitch had chosen a relatively shallow fording place and began transporting her pups one by one across it to an island in the middle. This island was not old but a product of a dividing of the river some fifteen years before, and the vegetation was young. The tallest growth was a stand of alder, and vine maple lined its sandy shore. This was their new home. They had crossed near a marsh of cattails and reeds formed in a backwater that had been partially cut off by the river's change of direction. Here male blackbirds flashed the red markings on their wings, while brown females grackled in the weeds. One bright male sat high on the brown tuft of a cattail and sang the wild song of his species. It was a sound that lifted upward into the intense blueness and brilliant sunshine of the sky.

An old, tom bobcat marked the wolves' arrival with disdain. He crouched hidden in a clump of salal brush and watched with bright yellow eyes. He had been on the island almost from its inception and was not pleased at the intrusion. Many a shrew and vole had filled his stomach from the rich harvest that shared the island. Now he must obviously leave, for the foraging pups would soon find his lair and bring their parents. He turned and slipped quietly into the marsh water. On the opposite bank he let out one nasty cough, a cry of protest, and was gone.

The bitch had undoubtedly chosen this spot in light of the increasing curiosity and restlessness of the pups. Here they were a little safer and more contained, though they had already outgrown the threat of the fox, the mink and the marten and all but the boldest of bobcats. Mountain lions, the only true enemies of a half grown wolf in this damp country that harbored no poisonous snakes, preferred on the whole the higher, more open country of the Olympic Mountain peaks. When they did venture into the low country, it was not in search of small game. All in all, the island was a good place, for it would restrain the movements of the pups while giving them greater range.

Now the parents were sometimes gone for days, and the pups supplemented their hunger with the small animals that had once supported the bobcat. There were men in this country, strong smelling creatures who used fish oils and seal fat to soften and glisten their tawny skin. But they were a people of the boat and the coastal sea, who rarely ventured inland into the dark, trackless forest toward the great mountain barriers. They kept their settlements near the salt waterways, mostly the Pacific Ocean but also Puget Sound. These men held an attraction for wolves because they maintained large rubbish heaps of discarded seal and fish viscera and other organic materials near the village encampments. Gray's parents knew of them, of a particularly large settlement by the ocean, and the time would come when they would move the pups again and locate them near the village. The rubbish heap would help carry them through the winter. For though deer and elk would also be in plentiful supply in the lowlands and many of the weak and sick among them would support the wolves, still the heap was a secure and ready food source always at hand.

That first summer is always the pleasantest time in a wolf's life, provided he survives it. The remaining four pups did that. They were of good stock and had intelligent, experienced parents who had raised several litters before them. Life on the island was sweet and carefree. And they did not always remain there. Sometimes one of the parents would take them back to the shore for the day to roam and learn to hunt small game in the dark woods.

The forest was indeed a very dark place, and breaks in its canopy were relatively rare, so small, sunlit meadows were few and far between. The great Sitka Spruces and hemlocks that dominated the canopy along with the huge, moss-draped maples of the Hoh valley seemed to shut out all hint of blue sky, and it was impossible to tell, just by looking, whether the sky was clear or overcast. Even the rain fell in occasional heavy droplets from leaves and hanging moss, rather than descend in the thick, stinging mist that came from the sky and blew in cold sheets in the late fall and early winter months.

Fall came with a cold, clear vigor. At six months, the young pups were like young sap in green trees, and they could not be restrained. Again and again they left the island, plunging into the cool, sun-fractured river to go off on their own or hunt with their parents. Gray was now the size of his sisters and showing signs of getting larger than they would. Though they were all of a tawny gray color, his coat had a deeper, smoky blue cast, and one of his sisters, the largest, was almost tan in lightness of shading. The other two sisters were nearly identical, one of them being distinguished by a darker shading in the hackles and a black tip on the tail. The parents were both lighter colored, tannish like the largest sister, so it was not immediately apparent where the darker shading had been inherited from. The pups were growing lean, adolescent, where their parents were heavy bodied, but they stood almost as high at the shoulders. Their yellow-green eyes, opening like slits above the slender muzzles and keen, white teeth, were a warning to all that these were young adults in the making.

The descent along the banks of the Hoh river to the ocean took several weeks, as the wolves were in no hurry. The weather was fine, clear and cool, warming to a comfortable sixty degrees Fahrenheit in the bright, sunny afternoons; and in the mornings a dense white fog hung over the river like incense or angel's hair. You could not see very far downstream through it, but the sunlight was caught up in it in brilliant shafts and pools of white light. When it lifted there was a sense that the river had been cleansed and that the day was starting out like the first day on earth.

The pups forged ahead of their parents, noses near the pebbles and sand along the margins of the river where the water had receded; their ears were erect and their eyes glistened with joy. Gray trotted along ahead of them all, snuffling at clumps of sedge and under boulders, depositing his scent markings as he went along. As each sister came to such a marking, she would pause to inspect it, then reinforce it with her own. The parents occasionally joined in the game, as if to give it their seal of approval, but, for the most part, they kept somewhat aloof, examining the winds, pausing to listen and look about.

Nevertheless, it was Gray who came across the bobcat they had forced off the island several months before. He immediately recognized the feline scent and bounded joyfully over to the quiet pool where the cat was crouched taking a drink. At first reluctant to move, the cat gave out a low moan, then retreated a few yards up the bank. On the one hand, he was in no mood to be chased off from his morning respite; on the other, a six month old wolf, however inexperienced, is a good sized opponent. Gray stopped to examine the warm patch of earth where the cat had been crouching. For several minutes he snuffed about as though unaware the cat was nearby, but, as it so happens with a curious animal, his sniffing happened to bring him closer and closer to the tom. Suddenly, with a snarl that sounded more like a snapping of giant fingers, the bobcat rushed down the wooded riverbank and charged the young wolf, his musclebound forepaws tearing at the earth like rods of iron. Gray yelped and leapt back out of range of the glistening teeth. Then they stood looking at each other, for the wolf did not know what to make of this ball of fury that was facing him now with a low, sinister moan. As the element of surprise began to fade, the wolf's hackles rose and a growl formed in his throat. The cat turned, fell back a few paces, stopped to find the wolf moving slowly toward him, ears laid back, then turned again and ran up into the forest. Gray did not pursue him, though he stood for several minutes facing tensely in the direction the cat had gone.

Tan, the largest sister, soon joined him, and Quick and Plain, the attractively marked and the unmarked pup respectively, were not far behind. Quick darted up into the trees, as if in pursuit of the bobcat but immediately returned to the communal investigation of the place where the cat had been. In the end, all left their markings and disdainfully departed.

Man is an interloper in the affairs of wolves, so the names chosen here have no romantic tinge. It is sufficient to know they are healthy young animals to give them all the beauty and meaning they need. In their natural state they know one another by smell and gesture. For no two wolves, any more than men, have the same personality. Gray exhibited a special degree of alertness and curiosity which may have been, at least in part, the result of his having begun life as the smallest member of the litter and consequently having to fight a little harder to get his share at the board. He was the most aggressive, yet, in some indefinable sort of way, the gentlest of the four. Tan, being the largest until Gray caught up with her in size, was also the slowest, stubbornest member of the litter. When very small, if she got hold of a teat, nothing could dislodge her, and her churning little paws would roll encroaching siblings away like barrels of refuse. Even now, once upon a small quarry or even pulling a tuft of grass, she would worry it into immortality. There was perhaps in her genes something of the primordial origins of the bulldog. Quick and Plain are adequately designated by their names, with this special note: Quick was not only fleet of foot and action but was of an unusual degree of high-strung nervousness. Plain was as solid and undistinguished as a banknote.

Now, the cause of their journey west, following the river, was, as mentioned before, the desire for added security, to remain in the vicinity of the garbage heap during the winter months. They did not subsist exclusively, or even extensively, on its contents but were always assured of its added support should game become unusually scarce. For this was that season of large prey and concerted effort when the wolves ran in small family-centered packs. In the softer months of the year, the parents had kept themselves and the pups going with an assortment of small game, like rabbits, muskrats, squirrels and mice. An occasional fawn or young doe brought satisfaction to the hunt and sharpened talents that never really grew dull. But even the deer were generally brought down by a single wolf acting alone or in concert with its mate. It was not until winter that they formed into the packs whose usefulness in bringing down the much larger elk was indispensable. And the garbage heap had through the years become a traditional rendezvous point for the interrelated wolves of the region to meet and form into these packs.

Gray and his family did not follow the river all the way to the ocean, but at a certain point of their journey made a northwestern exit into the forest. They had no trouble finding their way in the gloom of the sunless woods, as the two parent wolves were familiar with every moss and mushroom clad log, every moss hung tree, every trickle of clear spring water, and even a number of masses of rotting vegetation. For every natural compost pile has its own peculiar odor, every moss and fungus patch its special chemical nature. Though individual members come and go with the passing weeks, months and years, each moss and fungus patch is as unique in character as a family of wolves or humans. These things the wolves know, but they do not think about it. Thinking, in the rational sense, is a superfluous activity that man overcredits for his own progress in the world. The parent wolves made their way through the apparent tracklessness of the forest, not only through a keen sense of smell, but a sound memory that did not have to be called up in specific images, as men fancy, but which guided them almost unconsciously through intuitive impulses.

Men do much in this fashion as well, but will not admit to the fact. We pride ourselves on thinking our way through life, which we do not do, at least not as a rule. For most thinking is a mushroom atop the dying log of experience. It lives off the decomposition of memory, giving rise to intuitions we learn to use and reuse.

The wolves were also guided by hearing and sight. Wind blows a certain way at a certain pitch through different stands of trees on varying slopes of hills, and what little light enters the forest canopy comes in at a specific intensity and slant which varies like notes of music from place to place and season to season but is constant and recognizable in the same location at the same time of year. All this the pups learn by simply following their parents, doing what they do, and gradually becoming more and more attuned to their own impulses, repetitions and recognitions. Among men, when practiced to an exceptional degree, it is known as the sensitivity of the artist, the cunning of the woodsman and sailor. It is the fundamental character and practice of conscious awareness, the nature of sentient life.

The first snowstorm of the year arrived just as the wolves came to the ocean. The temperature was barely at freezing, and the snow fell in large flakes, which were not destined to stick for long. It is a wondrous sight to see six wolves trotting single file across a gray, stony beach rapidly going white from the snow. The huge, wet flakes would stick in their fur and immediately begin to melt, and now and then one of the wolves would stop and shake himself vigorously, driving the other members of the column out of line as they passed around him.

Gray found the ocean a subject of much interest. As the water receded down the beach he pursued it cautiously until a new wave would slap, foaming, uphill and chase him several yards. Through the curtain of falling snow, Gray could discern the large dull orb of the sun hanging low in the gray sky. Beneath it, fifty to a hundred yards offshore, the ocean rushed wildly against sentinels of rock that stood like columns in the waves, continuously showered in a spray of white foam. Atop some of these immovable piles of stone, amidst all the commotion, under the foulest of circumstances, hunched the implacable black figures of cormorants.

The tree line tumbles down to within seventy yards of the water line, then thins out into a dense, four foot high thicket of salal brush. The brush itself does not extend much beyond the trees and is replaced by coarse patches of sedge grass. After that the stones, white and dark, and slate colored sand extend on down until they slip under the roaring waves. The cataracts of foam made by the ocean swells dashing against the black sentinels of rock set up a continuous, deafening din. This is quite a different world from the stillness of the forest, and the wolves had soon retreated to the relative protection of the salal brush, where they darted about through the thick tangle of branches and stems in search of rodent fare. Out on the beach Gray took one last look at the gnarled, whitened trunks of old trees washed ashore, at the myriad of sea shells lying about among the stones, and at the brown, bulbous tubes and limp, green flotsam of seaweed. Then he caught a wood rat. Quick showed up to contest his possession of it. Having killed the rat with a crushing bite to its head, Gray retreated, snarling, to an especially dense tangle of brush and gulped it down as quickly as he could. Tan and Plain had ventured back out onto the beach and had wandered several hundred yards up the coastline together. The parent wolves were lying at rest in the salal near Gray and Quick. Out at sea, in the drifting snow and crashing foam, beneath the pale yellow-white disk of a forgotten sun, not a single cormorant had budged from its perch.

The human inhabitants lay somewhat to the south. Their village, with its long houses and sleek wooden boats, was situated in a small cove, protected on either side, north and south, by high sand cliffs, forested on top. In much of this northwestern Pacific Ocean country, the strip of beach is often slender, the land ending abruptly in cliffs, as if the endless forest suddenly ran out of room to grow. In storms, the waves beat upward over the narrow beaches, gouging the sandy cliffs. This creates uneasy footing for the outermost row of trees, whose roots are left exposed along the edge of the cliff. The next big windstorm brings them down. In time they will often be picked up by a rising tide and carted off to some other stretch of beach, where they whiten in the gray twilight of the mostly overcast coastal days.

The village, situated as it was, inside a cove, lay on a broader expanse of beach that extended to the cliffs on either side. These people were of little interest to the wolves, who avoided them and rarely stole into their camp and then only at night. What interested the wolves was the garbage dump located a little north of the dwelling area. Here brown and white gulls circled and jabbered, reeled, alighted, took off, fought each other, and landed again, squawking their piercing cries all day long. The wolves were here to socialize.

This might well have been called ammonia valley for the amount of marking with urine that was done. Each wolf made certain that every other wolf knew of his presence, for two different interrelated families of wolves came here to renew acquaintance every winter. As Gray's family approached the refuse heap for the first time that year, and, of course, for the first time in the lives of Gray and his sisters, they spotted three other wolves already at the site.

They approached cautiously. The wolves at the site turned to face them, ears flat, teeth slightly bared, tails drooped and extended almost straight behind them, a low growl emanating from their throats. Gray's father stepped forward from the knot the family had formed twenty-five yards off. He strode forward, hair bristling on his muscled back but showing no other sign of aggression, then paused about halfway between his family and the animals at the site. The three wolves at the site backed up a little in deference to the size of their interlocutor, for he was the largest wolf present. They repeatedly tested the wind with their muzzles, anxious to catch some news of who the newcomers were, but the wind was not right. They continued to emit low growls and began to pace about nervously. Gray's sire silently stood his ground, as Gray and his family stood motionless and looked on, each of them also testing the air for signs. In the stillness, the gulls had exploded into flight, and with their cries, their dipping and diving, reeled about overhead. A very light snow was falling, each flake finding its individual way to the ground.

Then a breeze picked up, very slight but growing stronger, and it began to push the flakes in a spiraling whirl toward the wolves on the mound, passing over the backs of Gray, his family and his father. The recognition was immediate. Catching the familiar scent, the three wolves at the site began to move about more freely, gently swaying their low hung tails and whining. Gray's father moved up and touched muzzles with the lead member of the smaller pack, a male, darker colored, looking somewhat like Gray himself, and not as tall at the shoulders as Gray's sire. This was Gray's six year old brother, a product of his parents' first litter. His two companions were his mate and a two and a half year old male, which was their pup.

Gray's father moved from the lead male to the other two wolves, inspecting them carefully. They were well acquainted. Gray and the rest of his family now trotted up and joined the general fray of friendly growling, whining, yipping, tail sniffing and muzzle biting. There were even mock challenges in which in a matter of moments the pack hierarchy was reestablished. This occurred primarily between Gray's father, the older son and the grandson, and immediately established Gray's father and mother in the leadership position as alpha male and alpha female of the pack. Gray and his sisters, being little more than whelps, knew their place as respectful adolescents. All this was accomplished to the din of harrying gulls in the twilight of early morning beneath the softly falling snowflakes. The pack would remain together for the winter.

The snow blew away with the rising sun, and the clouds broke to reveal a flaming red orb above the trees. The redness became orange, then yellow, as the sun mounted up in a blue sky. The heavy tree line stood like a black wall beneath the light, then lightened into a rich green. The pointed evergreens glistened with their powdering of snow. Above the forest canopy soared the occasional straight trunk of a dark green Douglas fir. The sky had now become intensely blue.

The first light storm of winter, lasting several days, had passed, and the remnants of the clouds that had caused it hung in billows near the base of the jagged, snow-capped peaks of the Olympic mountain range a few miles to the east. The ever gray ocean to the west now took on the blue lighting of the warm, yellow day. Even the waves did not seem as violent in their rush against the stone outcrops in their midst. Gulls from the garbage heap began to soar far and wide over the waves, and a flock of crows descended on the heap from the nearby forest. The cawing of the crows, the crying of the gulls, and the raucous jabbering of Steller's jays hopping from branch to branch in the trees of the forest, drifted across the beach to join the ocean's roar.

III

Winters in the lowlands of the Pacific Northwest are mostly a matter of rain. There is often an early snow in November and cold temperatures and snow off and on in January. But for the most part the days are a dreary succession of rain and sleet, driven by strong winds, sometimes of hurricane force. The strongest winds do much damage in the forest, felling weak, old trees to provide future nurse logs for the rows of seedling hemlock and spruce that will spring up along the decaying trunks. Along the beach, heavy winds pile waves into the sandy cliffs, creating much erosion, scattered debris and loss of trees there as well. Temperatures during the rains are relatively mild, hovering in the forties and fifties, due to the continuous cloud cover.

The elk, browsing all spring, summer and early fall on new growth high in the Olympics, return to the lowlands in the winter, driven there by the deepening snow pack on the glistening white peaks. In the lowlands near the coast there is plenty of foliage, and in those days little competition for it except from deer, who also move into the same country. The only major concern is the presence of wolves. The spring calves are large and fleet of foot; the fall rut is over. But there are always the weak, crippled by injury and disease. These are the ones who will fall to the wolves. It is a magnificent rhythm if one ignores the pain, fear and bloodshed that is the underpinning of natural life.

However, no living thing but man broods as man does. Reason is a sickness which scatters the powers of intuition before it. Had we not the ability to construct mighty bridges in time out of mere conjecture, could we not put a string of causational thinking together, the convoluted coils of which would tie a rattlesnake in knots, we would lead much simpler, happier, more effective lives. Death would come naturally and affect us only momentarily, as it does the wolf and the elk. In fact, it would seem that the end of all religion is to bring us through heightened trust, inner peace, and communion with the given order of things back to the subrational, animal truthfulness of the primordial human spirit.

A herd of thirteen elk had returned to their winter feeding ground within the hunting range of the nine member wolf pack. There were also many deer. The elk herd included eight cows, a bull, and four calves born the previous spring. The calves were all spritely and in good health, any weak stragglers having already fallen by the wayside in the summer and fall. They were as alert and fleet of foot as the best of the adults. But the cows were not so uniform, varying in age and fortune, some of them owing their continued preservation to their size. For a full grown cow elk can normally not only outrun a wolf but is almost as formidable an opponent as her heavily armed male counterpart in his finest autumn headgear. Her sharp hooves and nasty temper serve her well.

There was one very sick cow in this herd, the cause of whose malaise was not immediately apparent. When traveling she tended to follow at a distance of twenty to thirty yards behind the others. She looked patchy, not sleek in appearance.

Her eyes were glazed and dull, and she browsed or moved listlessly, refusing to stretch for the higher, more succulent twigs her companions could easily reach. Whatever her sickness, her fevered infirmity, she was a ready target for predators. The wonder of her not having already been taken was accounted for by the recent onset of her problem. So far she had simply not met up with any wolves.

There was also another injured cow in the group. She was the largest, oldest, and had been the lead cow until her accident. On the way down from the high country, the herd had come across a grizzly bear which had temporarily emerged from his long sleep during a warm spell. A cantankerous, mammoth, old male, he had challenged the elk for no good reason, roaring loudly, rising to his hind legs as they were passing through a clearing where he had been feeding on remnants of a wild huckleberry crop. The herd quickly moved out of his range and into the protective forest, but the cow had stopped to do her duty. She turned to face the bear, as a sort of rear guard, until all her retinue had escaped to safety. The bear had charged, his silver hackles flashing in the sun. The cow attempted to spring out of his reach at the last moment but was caught by a swipe of his powerful paw. He was not close enough to crush her spine and bring her down, but his sharp claws tore away some of the muscle in her left haunch. There were also cuts along her flank.

She got away with the rest, and the bear went back to his meager fare. But the wounds did not heal. They festered into sores, and she now ran with a limp, though she was not as weak as the sick cow.

The sick cow was, as might be expected, the first victim of the newly formed wolf pack. The elk herd was feeding in an open area wasted by fire then overgrown by salmonberry, blackcap, huckleberry, honeysuckle and salal. There were also a number of alder trees that had risen to an average height of four feet. It was a rainy December day, a day when the sky was depressingly overhung in a dark blanket of gray and the rain blew sideways in stinging sheets. It turned the matted fur of the elk as they browsed, but they were unaffected by the damp and cold. The wolves also ignored the inclemency of weather. In midafternoon they suddenly gathered in silence in the forest at the edge of the clearing nearest the elk. Since the wind was against them, they were not at first spotted. They moved about like shadows, slinking out into a line, peering with yellow eyes through the trees and brush at the ready meat.

The pack had formed a front line of the five adults. The four pups waited a little distance behind them, deeper in the woods. They would join in in the kill but would not attempt to bring down the quarry.

Do wolves know which individual is the weakest member of the herd? Not immediately, at least not always. They are opportunists and go for what they can get. As long as the wind held, they had plenty of time to observe.

The lead cow was the most alert. Another member of the herd had taken over the responsibilities of the injured one. There had been no quarrel or fighting displays to determine the new leadership, as would have occurred among the wolves or rutting bull elk. She who was next in strength, age, wisdom and endurance among the cows, who normally provide this leadership in the herd, simply assumed her inevitable role. Months, even years of traveling together for some of them had left no doubt as to who this was.

Before the wind shifted, the elk knew of the wolves' presence. The lead cow had detected movement in the brush along the line of tall evergreen trees. She turned to face into the danger, emitting a bark and raising her muzzle as if to test the wind. But the wind continued to blow steadily in the wrong direction. The herd began to gather behind her, moving together toward the opposite end of the clearing cracking underbrush and snapping twigs off the young alders as they walked through them. The lead cow stood firm and continued to face her undetermined adversary, her muzzle held high, nostrils flared, ears turning to catch any hint of further movement. Her eyes were large and wild. She stamped her left front foot several times in fear and challenge.

The wolves suddenly broke. Two young adults charged straight into the clearing, as Gray's parents and the third adult circled about to the right through the woods. They knew exactly what they were about. In the few seconds that had passed while the herd was gathering and pushing back toward the opposite end of the clearing, the wolves had detected the weakness displayed in the listless movements of the sick cow. It was enough to assure them that here lay their best chance of a kill. Each member of the hunting pack knew this simultaneously. The rushing tactic was automatically assumed by younger wolves, while the circling maneuver was left to older, wiser individuals.

The two rushing wolves had set the herd into panic. The lead cow also broke and joined them in flight. In seconds they were passing from the edge of the clearing into the woods, the sick cow trailing slightly to the rear.

The young adult accompanying Gray's parents caught the cow by the right haunch, clinging to her and acting as a drag.

She bellowed and attempted to break his grip in her panic. Gray's mother leapt toward her neck and grasped the underside of her throat. The first wolf lost his grip on the kicking hindquarter, the sharp hoof hitting him in the ribs. He yelped as he fell back but quickly resumed his hold. In these moments Gray's father grabbed the elk by the snout. With the combined weight of all three, she was toppled over. The minute she went down her struggle ceased, and the matter of tearing open her throat to let out the remaining energy of life was, in a sense, a simple surgical procedure. All nine wolves, including the pups, now piled onto the carcass and began eating pell-mell. When things grew a little crowded, several of the adults withdrew temporarily to let the pups get their fill. The rain swept over them in sheets, and the smoking, dark interior of the forest loomed nearby in the direction in which the elk herd had fled.

These wolves were not together at all hours of the day or on every day of the week. They often separated into the two original groups and spent short or lengthy periods apart. But they met regularly at the dump site, and the pressure of small game scarcity in the winter months, as well as simple affection, play, and the desire for companionship among closely related individuals, would reunite them. They met other wolves at the site too but did not join up with them.

The human inhabitants of the area rarely saw them but knew them by their eerie cries. Though they kept themselves far from contact with man, they had become the stuff of legend, and fear of them was one of the reasons these people rarely penetrated the deep forest.

On a clear night when a good moon was up to provide plenty of light and the stars were brightly shining over the pointed spires of spruce and Douglas fir in the evergreen forest, the wolves would sing. In a single, long, high-pitched howl, one of them would send the night across the forest like a cloak, and any creature caught out on that night would feel utterly alone. The cry would be answered by others, and soon several would be going at once from different parts of the forest. Sometimes this would serve as a method of rendezvous in lieu of meeting at a gathering point like the dump site.

Coyotes too filled the night with their barks and wails, and the calling of the wolves would sometimes be the thing to set them off. It was enough to make the dark, frigid air of winter seem forbidding and cruel. For both these predators get around well at night and are able to scent out the occasional sleeping deer and destroy it. Thus the sound of their voices sends a shiver through every still creature and sets to racing each tender beating heart.

Coyotes are considered pests by the wolves. Efficient hunters themselves, they are nevertheless prone to scavenging when this easier method of getting a meal is available. Many are the fresh carcasses they have stolen when the wolves' appetites were satiated and they had temporarily withdrawn from the kill. It is not easy to hide meat from coyotes, even by burying it, or by covering it as a mountain lion does, and for this reason, wolves are not tolerant of their smaller cousins. But, avoiding direct contact, the coyotes are never far away, and their less melodious yips and howls are a sign of their ubiquitous presence.

It was when the wolf pack brought down its second elk that winter that Gray lost another sister. For the eight month old pups had participated directly in the kill, and their clumsy inexperience, so much a part of learning, proved fatal to one.

They had not seen the herd for several weeks and had made no special effort to track it down. But the intuitive feel a wolf has for his environment is an uncanny thing. He knows much without having dwelt upon it. What this pack knew about the elk herd was that there was still infirmity among them. In time the knowledge of this infirmity drew the wolves back to them.

There is a freshwater pool which is the broadening mouth of a small stream that trickles through the low country and empties into an estuary of brackish water. The pool forms a small freshwater marsh at one end and is the home of teal and mallard in spring and summer. On the other side the water is clear of cattails and marsh plants and, running up against a low dike of firm soil, provides good access for thirsty animals. On a very cold, bleak morning the elk herd had come down to it and several of them stood pawing the ice with their sharp hooves until they broke through. The ice was never thick, for the weather did not remain below freezing for long periods.

On this morning, with the light beginning but the sun not yet up in a woolly sky and a sharp wind blowing out to sea, it began to snow. The snow came in large wet flakes at first but soon intensified into a gale of small ones. The snow swept out and covered the iced over surface of the pool in white, as it matted in the fur of the elk and frosted the cattails. A single crow flew down beside the elk to join them in its thirst. It drank for several minutes, dipping its bill into the water beside the brown, snorting muzzles then raising its head to swallow. It would close its eyes when swallowing, then fluff its feathers, stretch its wings, and caw loudly.

Suddenly it flew up and beat its wings back to the forest, cawing raucously. The drinking elk raised their heads, listened intently for a moment, and tested the biting wind for any unwelcome scent. The rising sun was making the sky a little lighter in the east and whitened the swirling drifts of snow. The snow was coming down heavily in twisting sheets which were thick enough to blot out sight of the nearby tree line of the forest. The wolves had circled down below the elk, where the keen eye of the crow had picked out their sliding movements. But the wind being in their favor and the snow muffling sound, the coming danger went completely undetected by the elk. When it exploded in snarling fury in their midst, they broke into the panicked confusion of head long, scattered flight.

In the first few decisive seconds the lame cow was singled out and isolated. The wolves had, without hesitation, closed in directly on her, one of them actually running out onto the ice and cracking through. This was Tan, and she let out a yelp as her heavy body plunged into the freezing water. Scrambling up onto the bank, she joined the rest of the pack, all nine members of which had formed a taunting circle around the cow. The herd stood closely packed near the edge of the forest, well out of reach but in visual range of the danger. From this safe distance, they watched the drama unfold. Now and then one of them would stamp indignantly but impotently, as all stood with ears erect, watching and listening in perfect silence.

Several of the wolves had sat down on their haunches, tongues lolling, in the circle that surrounded the wounded elk. Being an experienced old cow, she faced her adversaries with calm resolution. Every nerve of her body was alive with one desire: to get away. But she knew she was trapped, had faced danger a number of times in the past in her responsibility as lead cow, and knew that the only thing that could have put her in this predicament was her lameness. She had the nobility of the full grown animal that senses the extent of its powers and accepts their abatement with calm resignation.

The pups, being inexperienced, were the most eager to get on with events. Quick suddenly leapt from the waiting circle toward the face and throat of the cow, and in one quick snap the cow dealt a blow with a sharp forehoof to the pup's skull. Quick yelped, was flung outward by the force of impact, and lay lifeless, bleeding into the snow. Instantly the wolf pack closed in, snarling, snapping, grabbing hold of the elk at any available point. Gray, who had taken hold of the wounded haunch, tore away a hunk of muscle and flesh. The cow bellowed and struggled to remain standing, the wolves hanging all over her. Three of them were now tearing at her haunch, making a meal as she stood. Nostrils flaring, brown eyes bursting with pain and fear, the cow staggered and finally, from sheer added weight and fatigue, toppled over. A pair of powerful waiting jaws seized her throat and shut out life.

The wolves began to feed immediately; several members of the watching elk herd stamped and gave a snort, then they turned and slipped one by one, by graceful bounds, into the safety of the forest. The drifting snow, powdering the backs of the feeding wolves, soon covered and obscured the mound that was Quick's body. The sun was fully up somewhere in a gray blanket of sky, and a crow cawed from the woods. Perhaps it was the crow which had given the first warning.

IV

The month of February was almost a continual downpour. The rain did not always fall in buckets; it was often little more than a drizzle; but it came steadily from beneath cold, dreary skies. In this period the elk herd, now composed entirely of strong, healthy members, was of little use to the wolves. Deer were plentiful but a certain amount of luck was required to pick up the scent and come across one bedded down at night or during the midday hours. When this happened they usually bolted too quickly to be surrounded or caught. So the wolf pack often divided and foraged for snowshoe hare and other small game in the two original family groups. As it had for many years, the dump site near the village served as a rendezvous point and an extra source of food.

Other wolves came here also, because the site lay at the southernmost boundary of Gray's family range. That is why so much marking with urine was done: to reaffirm territorial limits. Otherwise the wolves were tolerant and friendly toward one another. It was common ground.

March was also wet and very windy and often found Gray foraging with his family along the beach. Much rodent life inhabited the salal brush and supplied the wolves with small but ready meat. The sea blew in cold, dashing the stone pillars offshore with its salty spray.

Affection is always keen among these animals, and during this period it becomes more marked between sexually active individuals, for it is the breeding season. Gray's parents began to separate themselves from Gray and his sisters for long intervals, sometimes lasting several days. On one such occasion they went far up the beach, leaving the pups behind and settling on a high wooded knoll overlooking the ocean. The female was in a state of agitation, whining when the male came near her. He, in his turn, was overcome with excitement. He trotted beside her, nipping at her shoulders, then dropped behind her several times to investigate her genitals. Finally reassured that she was receptive, he mounted her. Several times they repeated their lovemaking, then returned together to the beach. For awhile the knoll became a favorite retreat.

Shortly after this, the five wolves struck out for home. In late March the winds are fierce, uprooting trees on the edge of the forest and occasionally whipping the ocean waves into a fury, sending a mat of salt spray hundreds of yards inland beneath lowering skies. But deep in the high canopied woods, a busy peacefulness prevailed. Chickadees chirped, thrushes and winter wrens broke out in song, woodpeckers hammered, jays scolded, and an occasional Douglas squirrel chattered and whistled from overhead branches or moss covered rocks. The wolves were headed back toward the Hoh valley, catching mountain beavers, muskrats, rabbits, a few squirrels and chipmunks, and rooting salamanders from beneath the leaf litter and old logs for sustenance.

In the eternal twilight of the rain forest, with its ferns, occasional sapling trees, leaf, moss and evergreen needle floor, fungus, moss and seedling covered trunks of fallen trees, and the great clubmoss hairy arms of giant maples, the only indication of softening weather was a temperature change, an increasing balminess in the air. The sap began to run in the black cottonwoods and maples, which had lost their leaves in the winter, and the blood coursed a little more vigorously through the bodies of the wolves.

In May, back at the old den, the mother whelped, producing a small litter of four puppies. There were now more individuals to bring in food for the little family than there were helpless ones to consume it. But this was not destined to be a happy, productive spring like the former.

Perhaps it was the presence of a red fox family which had established itself nearby. Due to a prolonged winter chill in the deep interior of the Olympic mountain range, the spring meltoff was late as well, and the waters of the Hoh river were deceptively low. Either consideration may have led the mother wolf in her decision to move the pups when they were only a few weeks old. Whatever the reason, she transported them to the island, once again running off the bobcat which had reestablished itself there.

All the wolves were off hunting, except Gray. Gray's sisters, being superfluous since Gray had taken over most of the third parent functions, were often gone for days sharpening the skills that would soon give them independence and enable them to raise families of their own the following year. It was dark, very early in the morning. Both parents had gone off together and had not yet returned. When they left, the level of the river had already begun to slowly rise, but they had not taken note of it.

A close analysis by some careful observer would have shown an increasing buildup of silt in the water, indicating heightened erosion upstream from greater flow. There was also a lowering of temperature from the sudden increase in meltoff. The cause lay miles away in the high country near the snow packs. Here a warm air mass laden with moisture from the Pacific Ocean had come up against the cold snowy peaks and condensed into a mixture of snow and rain. The rain, pouring in unusually heavy torrents, like a tropical monsoon, had not only added directly to a considerable rise in the volume of runoff but was melting the snow packs. The rivers, swelled in width and gorged with muddy water, pressed down toward the ocean, rising in their beds, moving silt, even rocks, and tearing out trees along their banks, submerging islands and surrounding forest.

But, of course, this did not happen all at once, though it did come rather quickly and unexpectedly. Gray lay asleep, curled around the pups, who were tangled in a contented heap near his belly. The water had been encroaching on the island for some time but the wolves were secure and warm, out of reach of the light drizzle that fell in their vicinity. Deep in an underground burrow which Gray's parents had enlarged for this litter, they slept.

It was the sudden chill of cold water which awoke them. By this time a good part of the island was submerged. The river had risen several feet and was a raging torrent. Not only was the island almost entirely inundated, but the water had pushed out fifteen to twenty yards on either bank, enlarging the area Gray would have to cross to reach safety. At first trickling, the water soon poured into the den; and Gray found himself standing outside in the dark, surrounded by black water with one pup gently gripped in his mouth, while the other three lay drowning in the burrow.

It was immediately apparent to him that he had to get to higher land, but the cold, heavy rolling current was everywhere, swirling with fallen twigs and branches that lashed out in the darkness. Gray did not know where to ford the widened stream, but neither could he remain where he was. He plunged into the icy water on the north side of the island, which in normal times was the accustomed crossing point. Immediately, he was caught up in the strong current and swept downriver.

In panic he turned toward the north bank, paddling furiously, the pup still held firmly in his jaws. Against the night sky, he could see the pointed tops of the evergreens sweeping by. A large leafy branch, torn loose somewhere upstream, crashed into his right flank, thrusting sharp twigs beneath his muzzle and across his face. Never releasing his grip on the pup, he was turned about, facing downstream, and forced into a clump of red alder and scouler willow, which was all that remained unsubmerged of another small island.

Gray had taken quite a bit of water into his lungs. His aching limbs were growing numb from cold and exertion. But he held on to the pup. Pressing through the tangle of brush, he broke free and hurtled onward like a bullet. Paddling furiously, he turned again to face the north bank. The current carried him closer to the inundated tree line. The black trunks seemed to rush past him in a continuous line. Paddling more furiously until he hauled himself in among them, he felt the force of the current slacken. Then his feet touched the soft, slippery mud of the gently sloping bank beneath the water's flow.

It was difficult to stand up, for the water pressed against his chest, and even more difficult to move in the sucking mud. But little by little he hauled himself out of the river. Gaining dry land, he stood shivering among the trees. Gently he laid the pup on the leafy forest floor. It did not move. He nudged it with his muzzle, and a gurgle of water ran out of its slackened jaws. In bewilderment, Gray stood panting, shook himself and sniffed the cold form. Behind him the rushing river filled the night with its roar. The sky had begun to clear, and, through the thinner canopy of the forest near the water's edge, stars showed their white points of light, like cold jewels.

V

Having no responsibility but themselves, Gray's family ranged more widely that summer than they would normally have done. They left the Hoh valley and traveled deeper into the Olympic mountain range. For a time they worked the high country, favorite domain of the cougar, mountain goat and occasional black bear. They came there because the open alpine meadows with their clumps of twisted, wind blasted spruce, their green islands of fir, their fiery patches of red paintbrush and yellow buttercup, frequented by small clouds of rosy finches and the buzz of individual hummingbirds, were home of the ground squirrel, fat marmot, quick meadow vole and young deer.

Beneath patches of white snow, the meadow vole rustled about, quivering the stems of small plants that broke through. Hunting these active little animals was a pleasant way to spend an afternoon, though getting enough for a meal required no inconsiderable amount of work. An occasional marmot was nice and a fawn or kid was the desired prize. But the wolves did not often attempt the mountain goats, for they were agile climbers among the stony peaks. Their young were quick, coordinated, and astonishingly alert.

The wolves settled near a small alpine lake, green with algae, covered with breeding mosquitoes, and loaded with trout and minnow which broke the surface in small ripples in continual pursuit of the mosquitoes and their larvae. Though they remained loosely knit as a family, each wolf followed his own routine through the summer, usually hunting alone.

One morning Gray saw a golden eagle take a marmot. The eagle had been circling high above, and several marmots were feeding on a rocky slope. One marmot stood as sentry atop a large boulder. At first he did not seem to notice the eagle, but as the bird tilted its wings, made a wide circle and came in lower overhead, its shadow lengthened, and the sudden passing of it alarmed the marmot. He whistled and all the marmots were gone into the nearest rock piles. The eagle flew off and climbed up high in the bright, clear sky. Its shadow became less conspicuous and the marmots returned. The sentry resumed his post; the others continued feeding.

Far up in the blue expanse the eagle circled, neck extended below its body, head turning from side to side as it surveyed the miniscule scene below with its keen eyes. Even at this distance, with a small shadow, the eagle made the marmots nervous. Several times they darted beneath the protecting rocks. But as nothing happened they began to grow less wary. In the last rush for cover, one of them remained out in the open, ignoring the warning whistle. The eagle swung upward in the sky, turned in the west and, as this was midmorning and the yellow sun lay to the east, swooped downward at great speed, trailing its shadow far behind it.

The sentry whistled and dove as the eagle passed like a shot directly over him. Several marmots ran for safety. But in those crucial seconds the one who had ignored the previous warning hesitated. The sudden, crushing force of sharp talons entering his body like hooks of steel was too quick even for pain. The sunshine and pleasant herbal smell of the meadow became cool oblivion.

Gray's response had not been bold. He had flattened himself in the grass, ears laid back, as the eagle, with its seven foot wingspan, carried its victim off, emitting a wild cry. The young wolf had been observing from a short distance in an attempt to take one of the marmots himself. In fact, he had centered his interest on the very marmot the eagle took, noting, as the bird had, that it had developed a fatal indifference to immediate events. The broad wingspan of the great brown bird had made a keen impression, for here was something large and powerful which moved at tremendous speed and had the advantage of the air. But most important was the eagle's success in employing a kind of feinting tactic. Shortly after this the wolf was to attempt a use of this tactic in pursuit of larger game.

He had come upon a doe in a nearby meadow, accompanied by a pair of fawns. A number of deer grazed cautiously in the region in spite of the presence of the wolves. But they usually kept close to a clump of fir, feeding along the edge of it and moving from the vicinity of one copse to another in quick trots, ears erect and turning. In the predawn hours or at dusk they drank at the mountain lake, for the wolves were often active elsewhere then.

On this midmorning, several days after Gray's encounter with the eagle, the three deer were grazing quietly, unalarmed, as no wolves had been about since the evening before. Warm sunlight filled the meadow, and butterflies, large and small, yellow, brown, and white, fluttered about.

Gray came upon the scent of the three deer before he saw them, and he realized that when he rounded the copse of trees to his right, they would have him in sight. He trotted on, slipped into open view, and stopped. The mother flicked her tail, raising her head, and her young disappeared into the fir trees. Gray stood still as the doe nervously eyed him, lifting her nostrils into the wind, trying to catch his scent. He turned and moved off in the direction from which he had come. The doe went on cropping grass, and the fawns reappeared to frolic in the warm sunlight.

Again Gray showed himself, and again the fawns retreated, leaving their mother to attempt fruitlessly to catch a scent of the intruder. But the morning breeze, when it rose lightly now and then, remained in the wolf's favor. Gray did not attempt to advance beyond the point of showing himself, and soon went off again. His great advantage lay in a constancy of direction in the wind. Without this reinforcement of her conviction, the doe remained unsure as to whether or not the reappearing interloper was a threat to her and her young.

Finally, after several more feinting moves on the part of the wolf, she lost interest altogether and did not send her fawns to cover. Observing this increase of laxness, Gray made his last appearance at a dead run.

He had a fawn by the nape of the neck before it could respond to its mother's belated warning. She and the other fawn fled into the copse of fir. Gray threw all his weight on top of his prey, forcing it to buckle to its knees. It bleated once as its mother and sibling reappeared on the other side of the copse. The mother stopped, turning her ears to the sound. It was not repeated, and she and her remaining fawn bounded off through the adjacent meadow.

This was a summer for sharpening skills. Gray and his two sisters, Tan and Plain, achieved almost full independence but remained in frequent social contact with each other and their parents. In the winter they would reform into the close-knit family unit of the hunting pack and return to the seaside lowland along with migrating elk and deer. But for the summer, or the early part of it, they remained in the high country, an unusual event for them, as their normal range during the softer months lay in the Hoh river valley. Often on clear, starry nights, well above the cloud cover blanketing the rain forest, their lone howls could be heard.

The chief rendezvous point was the small, green mountain lake. There was an isthmus that extended thirty feet into the water and ended in a sort of attached island. Here they would often gather during the hottest hours of the day to rest. It was the period of least activity for most ground dwelling life, so it was a great time to loll about, sniff, whine, nuzzle one's neighbor, and sleep. It kept the family ties up at a time when each was taking care of his own needs alone and was therefore independent of the rest. Even the mother and father foraged separately, though they would occasionally share a meal that had been brought down by one or the other of them.

Mosquitoes abounded in the millions, swarming the air or moving in a continuously shifting mass over the surface of the lake. As the wolves lay sprawling in the mountain heather and wind blasted spruce of the rocky outcrop, mosquitoes came and went, setting up a continuous irritating hum and settling on the ears and muzzles of the wolves. Tan lay in just such a condition early one afternoon. Repeatedly she would raise her head and snap at one of the pests. But they were elusive little devils, quick, evasive, yet perishing in the serene indifference of overpowering numbers.

Green darners darted overhead, often in pairs, sometimes joined in the midst of flight. One such united pair caught Tan's attention, and she suddenly leapt up in pursuit of it. The dragonflies rose quickly and darted out of reach. Tan followed, slipping on a rock and plunging into the water. A cloud of mosquitoes rose then settled back again in a swarm about her nose as she paddled about. Nearby a trout popped the surface. Then another did the same. Tan turned around and paddled back toward land, as the dragonflies, now broken apart and flashing green and blue in the sun, one following directly behind the other, hunted mosquitoes off the island of her nose.

Tan regained the outcrop to be greeted by her curious brother, tail held low, swaying softly. Tan shook herself, showering Gray, then both settled down again to peaceful slumber. A pair of gray jays hopped about the rocks and heather, seemingly oblivious of the bevy of wolves into whose midst they had descended.

VI

Several large snow packs were in the vicinity, and their clear, cold runoff provided a refreshing alternative to the green water of the lake. This runoff ran in rivulets through sloping meadows to the forest margin. Not far beyond that a number of them joined to form a rocky pool that then ran off in a stream to join the Hoh in its valley. The rocky pool, being clear, cold, shallow, and oxygen rich, made an excellent spawning bed for salmon. In the height of summer, the great fish came there to lay their eggs on the gravelly bottom then die, exhausted by their long fight up the mountain through river white water and the narrow channels of the stream.

For many years an old grizzly had fished this pool, and he was there on the morning Gray and Tan came across it on their meandering return to the Hoh valley. They had left their parents and sister behind. These three would rejoin them later near the den site where the younger wolves had been born. From there in the fall they would journey to the ocean.

Presently the bear was fishing, standing well out in the middle of the spawning beds. He would lumber about, find a sluggish fish, spent from its final duty of egg laying, and break its back with his mighty paw. This was easy feeding, and the hungry wolves standing on the bank observed it with interest. They had returned to the forest due to the relative paucity of game in the alpine meadow. But, young and inexperienced though they were, they had enough sense to recognize a powerful adversary in the brown behemoth.

They stood for several minutes watching eagerly, sat and watched some more, mouths open and tongues dripping in the summer warmth. The bear worked slowly, methodically, killing a fish, then holding it down on a flat rock just beneath the surface of the water as he tore off mouthfuls of flesh. The moving water carried off the dark entrails in a stream. These traveled to the point where they met a beaver dam. There they broke up, eventually washed over the dam and went on downstream. This did not come to the attention of the two wolves at first. Neither did they notice with any particular interest that a grove of alder on the opposite bank was fronted by a line of pointed stumps, the work of beavers.

But as these things began to dawn on them, the wolves also noticed that chunks of meat, even a whole fish now and then, would be caught by the current and carried to the dam, out of reach of the bear. The two wolves inspected the dam site but found the matter of getting out on it to the point where the water carried its debris over the top no easy feat. They pondered this for awhile, trotting back and forth along the bank, until the satiated bear lumbered off into the forest. This emboldened them to enter directly into the shallower parts of the pool, and here, with much splashing and slipping on the rocks, they were able to capture a few of the spent and dying fish.

The following morning the bear returned and began fishing again in the exact spot he had occupied the day before. The wolves watched for some time, then suddenly got up and moved downstream, as if no longer concerned with proceedings in the pool. They trotted into the woods for some distance and busied themselves with sniffing under logs and the moss laden rocks. Eventually they reemerged well below the dam at a point where the water flowed gently only a foot deep over a broad expanse of gravel and sand. Stepping out into the bone chilling current, it was an easy task to retrieve the chunks of meat that floated down from the pool. For as long as the bear and spawning fish remained, the wolves were well supplied. It was a larder capable of sustaining them for several weeks.

Rich in fish oil, sleek of coat, and keen of eye, Gray and Tan once again resumed their journey through the dark, musty forest. No yellow wash of sunshine broke the shadowy stillness. Straight, rough barked trunks of fir, spruce and hemlock rose high above them to close their branches overhead. They caught chipmunks and were scolded from the trees by the squirrels. Woodpeckers knocked and flights of black-capped chickadee scattered past them in noisy flocks, dozens of the little birds perching at every conceivable angle on the out-flung branches and their twigs.

The old den was there, still unoccupied, lying fallow, as it were, for a season. The island too rose bright and clean above the rushing waters of the Hoh river. Gray crossed over to it, while Tan remained preoccupied in the adjacent forest. Gray found the entrance to the island den still covered with the debris of twigs and brush left by the flood. Inside there was no sign of what might have become of the drowned pups.

Within a few days, the family of five was reunited. Reestablished in a territory that, after a thorough search for scents and a remarking of boundaries, did not appear to have been violated by more than an occasional passing wolf, they settled in for the remainder of the summer. There was much game in deer and smaller quarry, and a family of raccoons that hunted crayfish in the nearby creek lost a careless youngster to these wolves. The raccoons' chittering could be heard often for some distance in the night, and the endless growls and scufflings of the half-grown cubs reverberated through the woods from the creek and river banks. In daylight crows would sometimes gather in angry flocks to harass the sleeping wolves, and raucous Steller's jays would hop from branch to branch in the willow and vine maple along the sun washed riverside.

Fall found them once again in the coastal lowland. Here they rendezvoused with the family of wolves they had formed a pack with the previous winter. That family had changed its composition. The young male was gone, and in his place were four pups born that spring: two females and two males. There was less snow that winter and the numbers of deer and elk seemed fewer, perhaps because the snows were not as heavy in the mountains and had not driven them all as far as the coast. So the wolves often hunted in smaller bands and subsisted largely on rodents, large and small, and scraps retrieved from the trash site north of the human settlement. Though hunger sometimes drove them to the edges of the village, they never entered it, for they were wary of man, having from time to time seen him hunt in the neighboring forest and knowing him for a wily predator. But these were a seafaring people and such occurrences were generally rare.

Spring brought its tender urgency to the relationship of Gray's parents and saw to the departure of his two remaining sisters. In sexual heat they wandered off and soon found mates. In May Gray returned to the den site along the Hoh river with his parents. It would be another year before he left them.

A litter of eight was born and all survived, so his help was much needed. In the first few weeks the mother never left them, while Gray and his father ranged far and wide to collect the sustenance which they brought back in their bellies and regurgitated for the female's consumption. When the pups' eyes had opened and they began to wobble on their stubby legs, the female returned to hunting and Gray took her place as guardian in the den. Because there were three adults, the litter was almost never left unguarded, which greatly increased the odds in favor of its survival. The winter's snowfall having been lighter than that of the previous year, the riverbeds were better able to handle the spring runoff, and there was no serious flooding. Never in their lives had Gray's parents seen a flood like the one of the year before. Their memory of it was enough to keep them off the island all summer.

It was a large wolf pack that formed in the coastal valley the next winter, though many of its members were inexperienced hunters and not fully grown. This placed a heavier burden on the adults, and they ranged long and lean throughout their hunting territory. Every living thing was made to know by the lone, chilling, wolf calls of the omnipresent urgency and danger.

VII

Gray's fourth spring coursed through him like molten fire and drove him far away from all the wolves he had ever known. It was wet, rainy almost every day, and the wind roared along the coastal beaches, bringing salt spray in as far as the forest edge. Gray wandered up and down the beaches, subsisting on whatever meager fare he could find. He was not terribly hungry but was consumed with physical longing. His occasional forays along forest trails brought him scent signals of the presence of various canidae, of coyotes and a few wolves. But his search did not end until he had traveled a considerable distance up the coast. There, along a stony beach, he picked up the markings of a young female in estrus.

She was two years old, a lighter gray with white markings about the face and slightly smaller than himself. Having caught the scent of her condition, he found her tracking solitary in the wet sand along the water's edge. He trotted up behind her with a growl, tail swaying lightly. She turned, snapped at him, ran off several yards, and stopped. He approached again, sniffing her genitals, licking them. She turned around and sniffed him.

For several minutes the inspection went on with an eager insistence. Then the tension subsided, and they began frolicking and nuzzling one another, running up and down the wet, sandy beach together through the harsh wind and the cold, salt spray. Forty-eight hours passed before they mated, and Gray's first attempts to mount the female were clumsy. She was no help herself, for in her excitement she suddenly ran off, leaving him sitting bewildered on the sand. Eventually sexual union was consummated, and the whines and yelps that drifted faintly along the beach through the roaring blast spoke of new life that would soon begin.

They mated repeatedly throughout the female's period of estrus, and for a little over a month remained together on the coast. Then they turned inland to build a den beneath a large rock deep in the gloomy forest. Though they both dug out the tunnel and the sleeping chamber, the female took the lead. She seemed in a hurry to finish the work, and within a week of its completion her time arrived.

A very small litter, only three pups, was born: two males and a female. It was not an easy delivery. Driven to a sudden panic from the unexpected pain, the female left the den and raced about outside, dropping young as she went. When it was over, she and Gray found the pups and licked them clean. After this, she carried two of them into the den. The third one, the female pup, never showed any sign of life.

Spring is softer in the woods, where the thick canopy formed by the trees mitigates the thrust of rain. But the shift to summer weather is hardly noticeable. The woods are always cool and pleasant, even during the hottest days of July or August. Gray and Whiteface, for so we shall call the female, were model parents after the initial shock of producing pups. Having only two to care for seemed to increase their devotion. Whiteface went a full four weeks before she would leave them to hunt. The den was located near a stream and Gray worked hard to feed himself and his mate, so her needs were well provided for. She rose once in the morning to drink and urinate, taking the time to inspect and freshly mark the immediate environs of the den. Then she would return, curl about the pups and suckle them. Sometime in the afternoon she would rise and repeat the process. When the pups soiled the den, she cleaned both them and the den, for wolves are tidy, affectionate parents. Her long, warm, gentle sessions in grooming her young encouraged them to suck and defecate, and provided them with a secure sense of being.

Gray was an excellent father also, and after the first month, frequently took the place of Whiteface in caring for them. Thus both parents shared in food procurement and nursery chores, as their parents had before them. But Gray did most of the hunting, since he could not nurse the pups. This function limited Whiteface in the duration of her forays, until the pups were weaned. Nights were the usual hunting hours, and from far away, amid the calls of other wolves, Whiteface would recognize the voice of her mate and crawl out of the den to answer him. They would then sing a resounding duet in counterpoint for as long as twenty minutes. First light brought Gray home, and, practiced hunter and forager that he had become, he promptly regurgitated for his mate the morning repast he had carried for miles in his stomach.

The pups grew strong and sleek, having the entire smorgasbord of their mother's belly to divide between them. Their fur was a bluish gray, like their father's, but one of them had much black in his coat as well. It darkened his face and was particularly noticeable in the broad strip that ran the full length of his back and tail. This was "Forest Demon," whom the people of another coastal village named in later years for his occasional but harmless appearance about their camp in the winter months. His dusky form lit by burning yellow eyes became the stuff of legend, embellished far beyond his natural means. His brother we shall call Dancer, for he was a very energetic fellow and often wore his slightly larger, heavier brother to a frazzle with his constant need for play. He would nip at him and tumble over him for hours, until Forest Demon lay exhausted on the ground. But both were strong and keen.

When the pups were six months old, the four wolves made the journey west, as Gray had done every fall. On the coast they had no rendezvous point, so they began to hunt and forage along the beaches without benefit of reinforcements. They had no knowledge of the village that would later attract the interest of Forest Demon.

It was well into the coldest month that their luck changed. Having no attachments and no settled territory for the winter, they had gradually drifted north to a headland that jutted out above a cove. This promontory was entirely covered with pointed fir and cedar. The three ocean-bound sides of it dropped off vertically in sandy cliffs rooted in a thin sill of sandy beach. The tree cover on the headland was, as usual, dense up to the very edges of the cliffs, and this served well to protect the wolves from the salt spray hammering the beach fifty feet below. The wolves therein had close access to both sea wrack and adjacent forest, while avoiding an endless dampening from the spray. Deer were plentiful and elk numerous, for though there was little snow, the unusual cold of that year seemed continually to threaten it. But, with only two grown wolves available for the hunt, Gray and his family were generally reduced to the pursuit of smaller game.

In the early morning, with a fog hanging low and a pale yellow sun breaking over the tree line to the east, the wolves could more often be heard than seen. For the pups had not yet developed the quiet, stealthy ways of their parents. Forest Demon might be the first to spot a wood rat in the thick brush along the upper side of the beach near the cove. Plunging into the thicket to grab it, he would create such a commotion his brother would be attracted and try to steal it. Dashing back and forth, growling and cracking bushes, Forest Demon attempting to eat his catch before he lost it, with Dancer at his side nipping and shoving, they would create a sufficient enough uproar to attract curious sea gulls. Wheeling and crying overhead, the birds' excitement marked the scene and cleared out all the game for hundreds of yards around. Thus, as a serious fisherman avoids a noisy crowd, Gray and Whiteface disappeared for hours at a time to hunt in peace, leaving the younger wolves near the beach.

Their first contact with a neighboring band of wolves occurred on such an occasion. There were five individuals in the band, all adults, the youngest being a two year old who had become the alpha female by dint of joining up with a strong, six year old male who had lost his original mate the previous summer. Two of the wolves in the group were much older, still being good hunters but waning in strength. These were the parents of the alpha male and a younger male sibling.

Now, though there is much growling and display, even among well acquainted pack mates, wolves do not often fight to the point of serious injury. Yet the threat of it is always there.

Gray had crossed the path of the alpha male on a trail in the forest. Whiteface was not far away and had suddenly become alert when the low whisper of a growl reached her ears. She caught the stranger's scent and rushed to join her mate. Not more than a few yards apart in a small clearing near the trunk of a large cedar that had been toppled by a storm, the two males faced each other. Their tails were lowered, fangs bared, hackles raised, yellow eyes gathered into slits, and the soft, guttural menace of their deep throated growling broke in coughing rasps.

For several moments they held one another at bay; then Gray, young and eager, charged. Reared on hind legs, the two wolves slammed into each other, growling and biting at the face and throat.

Whiteface stood and watched, hackles raised, a low growl rumbling in her throat. She saw her mate thrown back by the superior weight and strength of the older wolf. Twice the combatants broke apart in this manner, and Gray, recoiling, threw himself at his opponent with renewed fury. But finally realizing he was outmatched, he chose to yield. With a sharp yip, signalling his despair, he broke away from the larger wolf. When the latter charged, Gray bared his throat. This gesture stopped the alpha wolf, who with sudden gentleness accepted his submission.

Sniffing, whining, gently swaying their drooped tails, the three cemented their acquaintance. The alpha wolf had been foraging alone. He now left to rejoin his band, as Gray and Whiteface returned to their pups.

It was several days before the bands were united, meeting on the same forest trail. All readily accepted the leadership of the alpha male and female. It was a large and vigorous pack, numbering nine healthy individuals, only two of them pups. Though unusual in that it joined unrelated family groups, it proved a viable alliance and formed again over several winters, after which the leadership passed to Gray and Whiteface. In the long nights of many winters, their haunting calls could be heard, until encroaching man, untold generations later, drove their numbers from the forest.

Even now in the green darkness of that rugged, water enriched land, when the rutting elk whistles, the coyote howls, and a fleeting deer steals across a manmade road beneath the looming cedar, hemlock and towering Douglas fir, the ghostly presence of wolves and grizzly bear can still be felt. Except for puma, who lie hidden in the rocky peaks, these great predators are gone, but the mountains, topped with snow, remember them.

* * * * *